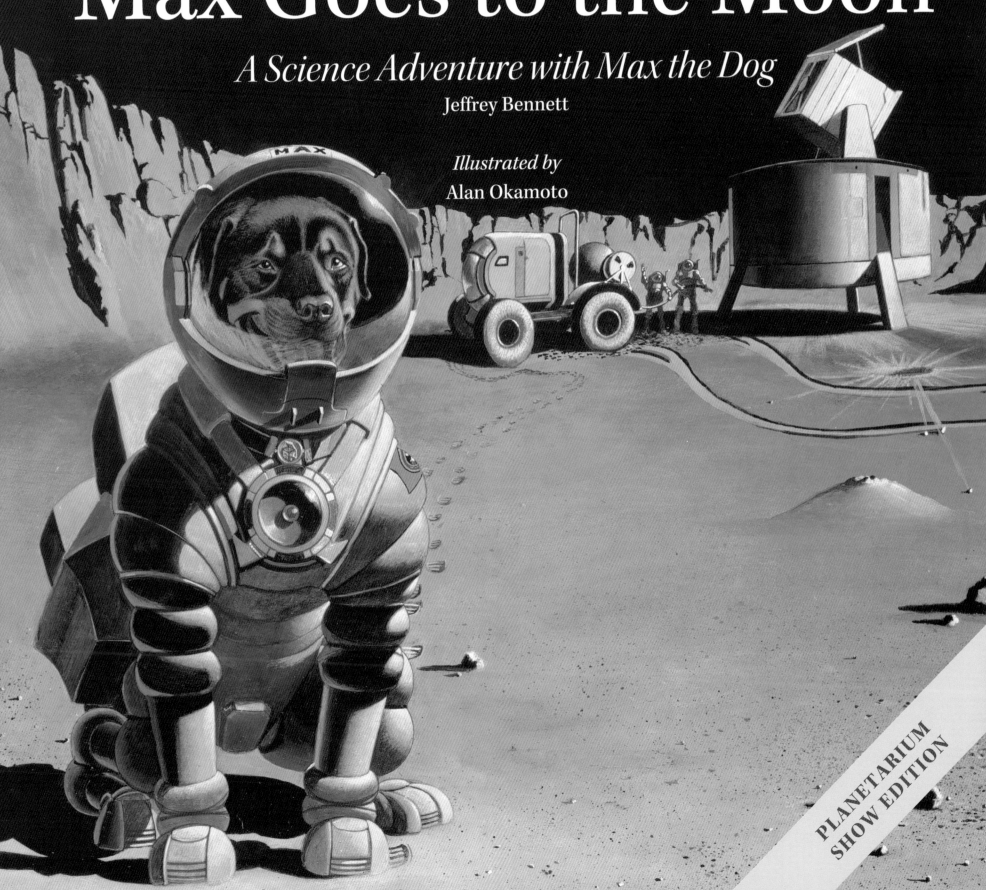

Max Goes to the Moon

A Science Adventure with Max the Dog

Jeffrey Bennett

Illustrated by

Alan Okamoto

PLANETARIUM
SHOW EDITION

About the New Edition

This new edition of *Max Goes to the Moon* is designed to accompany the multimedia *Max Goes to the Moon* planetarium show, now available to planetariums around the world. Although the basic story is unchanged, you'll find a new Preface and a substantially revised set of Big Kid Boxes, designed both to bring the contents fully up to date and to answer questions the author has been asked while presenting *Max Goes to the Moon* to assemblies at more than 100 elementary schools.

Editing: Robin J. Heyden, Joan Marsh
Design and Production: Mark Stuart Ong, Side By Side Studios

Published in the United States by
Big Kid Science
Boulder, Colorado
www.BigKidScience.com

ISBN: 978-1-937548-20-9

Also by Jeffrey Bennett

For children:
  Max Goes to Mars
  Max Goes to Jupiter
  Max's Ice Age Adventure (with Logan Weinman)
  The Wizard Who Saved the World

For grownups:
  On the Cosmic Horizon
  Beyond UFOs
  Math for Life

Textbooks:
  The Cosmic Perspective series
  Life in the Universe
  Using and Understanding Mathematics
  Statistical Reasoning for Everyday Life

Expert Reviewers

Dr. Thomas R. Ayres, University of Colorado
Dr. Laura Danly
Dr. Megan Donahue, Michigan State University
Dr. Erica Ellingson, University of Colorado
Angela M. Green Garcia, NASA Johnson Space Center
Dr. Susan Lederer, NASA Johnson Space Center
Mark Levy, Educational Consultant
Dr. Gary Lofgren, NASA Johnson Space Center
Dr. David S. McKay, NASA Johnson Space Center
Dr. Cherilynn Morrow
Dr. Nick Schneider, University of Colorado
Dr. Mary Urquhart, University of Texas, Dallas
Dr. Mark Voit, Michigan State University
Dr. James C. White, Rhodes College
Jonnie Lynn Yaptengco, NASA Johnson Space Center
Helen Zentner, Educational Consultant

Special thanks to Maddy Hemmeter as Tori

To Children Around the World:

Follow your dreams, study hard, and someday you'll live in a world as wonderful as the one we imagine in this book.

3

A Note from the Author

Astronaut Eugene Cernan, driving the "Moon buggy" during the Apollo 17 mission. No one has visited the Moon since Apollo 17 left on December 19, 1972. Isn't it time we go back?

The Apollo 11 plaque on the lunar lander, photographed preflight.

Imagine that you could send a single short message through time to anyone who has ever lived, telling them one modern fact that would give them hope for the future. I don't think you could find anything more powerful than this: Human beings have walked on the Moon, and upon first arrival left a plaque that read "We came in peace for all mankind."

No other single event in human history would be both so understandable — after all, everyone can see the Moon — and so amazing at the same time. For most of history, a trip to the Moon would have been considered impossible. Even once it became possible in principle, few believed that it could really be done. But not only did we do it, we did it in a way that made it belong to all of humanity, not just to the astronauts who made the trip, or to the people who built the program, or to the nation that paid for it. Surely, if we are capable of that, it would seem that we are capable of anything.

From 1969 to 1972, a total of 12 human beings walked on the surface of the Moon, but no one has been back since. Some people think this makes sense, because we have plenty of problems that we need to solve here on Earth. But I believe we'll be far better able to solve our problems if we have the inspiration that only exploration can provide. Imagine that, as in this story, we build a place where people from around the world can work together on the Moon. Every child, in every nation, will then be able to look up at the Moon in the sky and say, "We are working together up there, so surely we can work together down here."

That is why I believe it is time for us to go back to the Moon, and then onward to Mars, Jupiter, and beyond. In fact, I believe our future depends on it. I hope you'll join me, and Max, as we…

Reach for the stars!

— Jeffrey Bennett

This is the story of how Max the Dog helped people return to the Moon — this time, to stay.

It all began on the morning of the parade. Max had just returned from his trip to the Space Station. He was a hero, and everyone wanted to celebrate his adventures.

As Max's car drove along Pearl Street, Max looked to the west, and he began to howl just as the Moon set over the mountains.

Phases of the Moon

Look at the Moon setting over the mountains in the painting. Do you know what we call the Moon when it looks like this?

The Moon's cycle of phases goes from new (when we don't see the Moon at all) to full and back again in 29½ days, or about a month (think "moonth"). The diagrams below show the basic phases. The phases from new to full are all called *waxing*, which means "getting fuller." The phases from full to new are *waning*, which means "getting less full."

The waxing phases begin with a *waxing crescent* moon, then progress to *first quarter*, when we see exactly half of the Moon's face, and on to *full* moon. The waning phases continue in reverse, moving to *third quarter* and then to the *waning crescent*. If it seems strange that what looks like a "half-moon" is actually called first or third quarter, it's because we see the "half-moon" when the Moon is one-quarter or three-quarters of the way through its cycle.

Now, look at the phases in between the quarters and full, when we see most but not all of the Moon's face. These phases are called *gibbous* (which means "hunchbacked"), pronounced with a hard g as in "gift." The Moon in the parade scene is a *waning gibbous* moon, because it has the gibbous shape and comes after full moon.

Do you want to know *why* the Moon goes through phases? Try the activity on page 30.

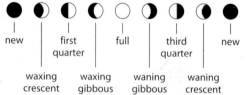

new	first quarter	full	third quarter	new

waxing crescent	waxing gibbous	waning gibbous	waning crescent

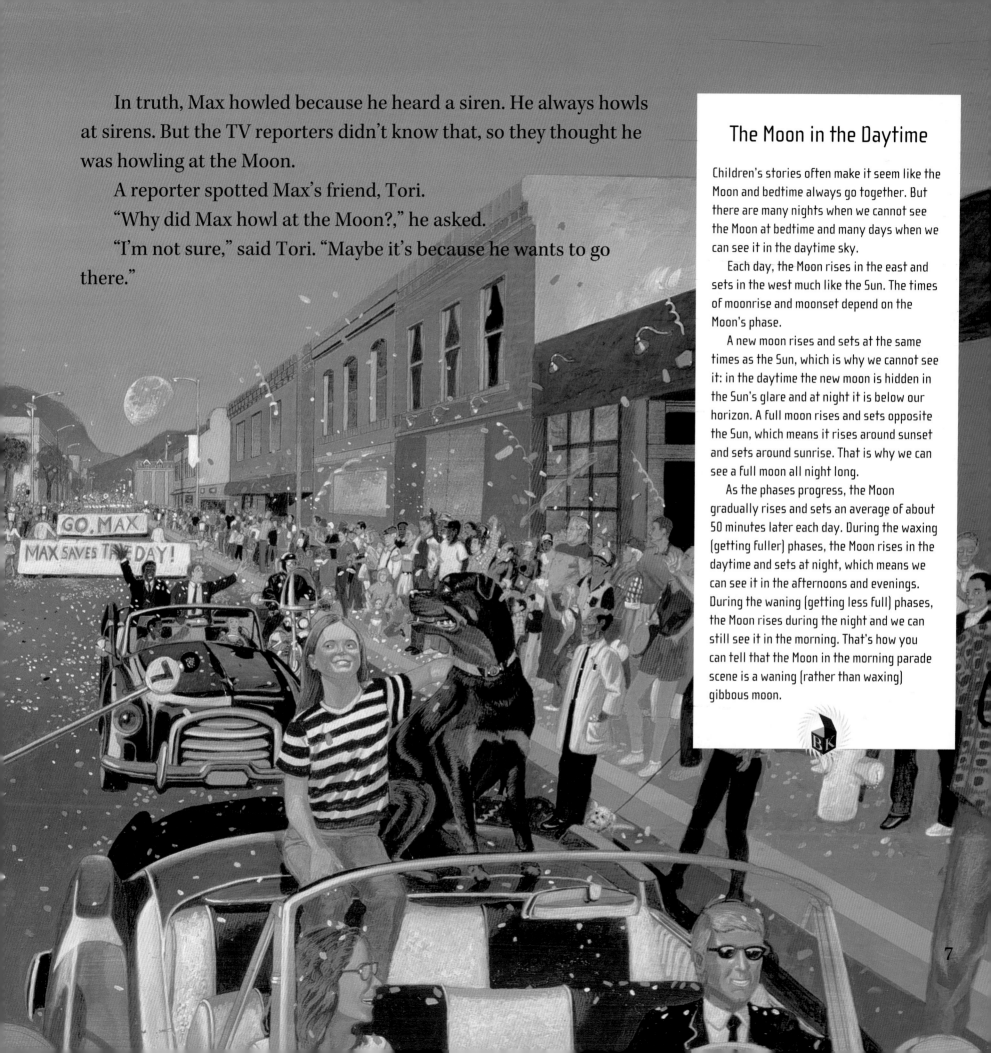

In truth, Max howled because he heard a siren. He always howls at sirens. But the TV reporters didn't know that, so they thought he was howling at the Moon.

A reporter spotted Max's friend, Tori.

"Why did Max howl at the Moon?," he asked.

"I'm not sure," said Tori. "Maybe it's because he wants to go there."

The Moon in the Daytime

Children's stories often make it seem like the Moon and bedtime always go together. But there are many nights when we cannot see the Moon at bedtime and many days when we can see it in the daytime sky.

Each day, the Moon rises in the east and sets in the west much like the Sun. The times of moonrise and moonset depend on the Moon's phase.

A new moon rises and sets at the same times as the Sun, which is why we cannot see it: in the daytime the new moon is hidden in the Sun's glare and at night it is below our horizon. A full moon rises and sets opposite the Sun, which means it rises around sunset and sets around sunrise. That is why we can see a full moon all night long.

As the phases progress, the Moon gradually rises and sets an average of about 50 minutes later each day. During the waxing (getting fuller) phases, the Moon rises in the daytime and sets at night, which means we can see it in the afternoons and evenings. During the waning (getting less full) phases, the Moon rises during the night and we can still see it in the morning. That's how you can tell that the Moon in the morning parade scene is a waning (rather than waxing) gibbous moon.

GO, MAX.

MAX SAVES THE DAY!

7

Leaving the Earth

If you throw a ball into the air, it falls back to the ground. But the harder and faster you throw it upward, the higher it goes before coming down. If you had magical strength, you could throw a ball so hard and so fast that it would never come back down. We would say that you gave the ball *escape speed*, because it went upward fast enough to escape from the Earth and go out into space.

The escape speed from the Earth is very fast — about 40,000 kilometers per hour (25,000 miles per hour). That is much faster than anyone can really throw a ball. It is faster than any airplane travels. But big rockets can go that fast.

Well, Tori's "maybe" was good enough for TV. By the next day, Max's dream of going to the Moon was all over the news. And because no one had been to the Moon in a long time, it seemed like it was about time for someone — or some dog — to go.

DAILY WORLD NEWS

MOON-DOGGY DOG

MOON

K-9 COURAGE

It's not easy to go to the Moon. It takes big rocket engines to get a spaceship off the Earth. It takes careful planning to make sure the astronauts reach the Moon and come back safely. And it costs a lot of money.

But everywhere Max went, crowds chanted, "Send Max to the Moon!" People wrote letters to the President. So a new moonship was built and assembled at the Space Station.

A Trip to the Moon

This story envisions a trip to the Moon that includes a stop at a space station, but that's not the only way to get there. The Apollo missions of the past took astronauts directly from Earth to the Moon, and many plans for future trips also call for direct flights.

The main advantage of a space station stop is that we could use the same moonship over and over. The most difficult and expensive part of a space mission is getting off the ground, and the heavier the spaceship, the more it costs to launch. By docking a reusable moonship at the space station (it's the round part with four legs near the bottom of the painting), we avoid the cost of launching it multiple times. Assembling the moonship in space may also save money, because it can be cheaper to launch several small rockets (each carrying part of it) than one very large one.

One important idea to keep in mind: No matter how we do it, a trip to the Moon is a much bigger trip than one to our current space station, which orbits Earth at an altitude of less than 400 kilometers (250 miles). The Moon is nearly 400,000 kilometers away, which means it is about *1,000 times as far* from Earth as the space station. To scale, the difference between going to the space station and going to the Moon is as great as the difference between a walk across Central Park in New York and a walk across the United States!

9

Tori gave Max the good news. "You are going to go to the Moon," she said. "I sure hope they let me come with you."

Why is the Moon a "moon"?

We call the Moon a "moon" because it orbits the Earth; any object that orbits a planet is called a moon (or *satellite*). But aside from its orbit, the Moon isn't so different from a planet.

Eight objects in our solar system orbit the Sun and are large enough that we call them *planets*: Mercury, Venus, Earth, Mars, Jupiter, Saturn, Uranus, and Neptune. Smaller objects that orbit the Sun and are still round in shape, such as Pluto, Eris, and Ceres, are called *dwarf planets*. Our Moon is smaller than the smallest planet (Mercury), but larger than any known dwarf planet.

The Moon is similar to a planet not only in size but also in composition. Like the four inner planets (Mercury, Venus, Earth, and Mars), the Moon is made almost entirely of rock and metal. In fact, planetary scientists usually think of the Moon and the inner planets together as our solar system's five *terrestrial worlds*; the word *terrestrial* means "Earth-like" and is used because all five worlds have rocky surfaces like Earth.

Earth	Moon
diameter = 12,760 km	diameter = 3,480 km

These photos show the sizes of the Earth and Moon to scale. To show the distance between them on the same scale, you'd need to separate the two photos until you could fit about 30 Earths between them.

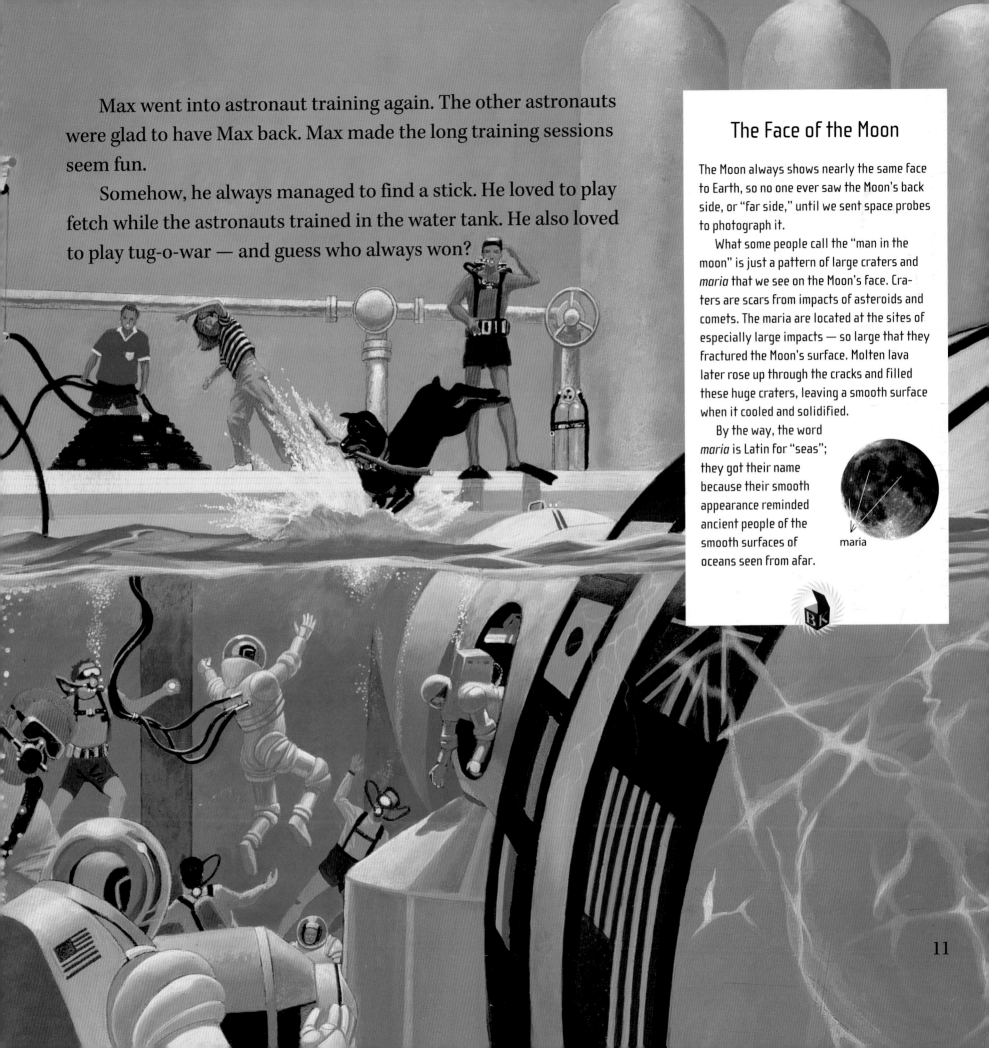

Max went into astronaut training again. The other astronauts were glad to have Max back. Max made the long training sessions seem fun.

Somehow, he always managed to find a stick. He loved to play fetch while the astronauts trained in the water tank. He also loved to play tug-o-war — and guess who always won?

The Face of the Moon

The Moon always shows nearly the same face to Earth, so no one ever saw the Moon's back side, or "far side," until we sent space probes to photograph it.

What some people call the "man in the moon" is just a pattern of large craters and *maria* that we see on the Moon's face. Craters are scars from impacts of asteroids and comets. The maria are located at the sites of especially large impacts — so large that they fractured the Moon's surface. Molten lava later rose up through the cracks and filled these huge craters, leaving a smooth surface when it cooled and solidified.

By the way, the word *maria* is Latin for "seas"; they got their name because their smooth appearance reminded ancient people of the smooth surfaces of oceans seen from afar.

maria

The Apollo Moon Landings

The painting on these pages shows what it really looked like when the Apollo 11 astronauts visited the Moon in July 1969. Notice their lunar lander, which was named the *Eagle*.

Astronauts Armstrong and Aldrin spent less than 24 hours on the Moon's surface. Meanwhile, a third astronaut, Michael Collins, orbited the Moon in the *command module*. When their mission was over, the top section of the lunar lander (the grayish part in the painting) blasted off and took Armstrong and Aldrin back to the command module, and all three astronauts traveled home together. Their entire trip from Earth to the Moon and back took about eight days.

Over the next three years, five more Apollo missions — Apollo 12, 14, 15, 16, and 17 — landed successfully on the Moon. (Apollo 13 had an accident in space that prevented its planned Moon landing, but the astronauts returned home safely.) No one has ever traveled farther. That makes a total of six Moon landings, each with two astronauts, which means that in all of history, *only twelve people have ever walked on another world*... so far.

Tori thought that Max should know a little history before his trip. So she told Max about the first astronauts who went to the Moon.

"Listen carefully, Max. Neil Armstrong and Buzz Aldrin were the first people to walk on the Moon. Their mission was called Apollo 11. They landed on the Moon on July 20, 1969. Neil Armstrong stepped out first. Do you know what he said when he took his first moon step?"

"Armstrong said:

That's one small step for a man,
one giant leap for mankind.

"Do you understand, Max?"
Max barked, and Tori took that as a "yes."
"Good boy, Max," said Tori.

About That Flag

Take a look at the flag. It looks like it's waving in the wind, but you probably know that it can't be. After all, the astronauts need spacesuits because there's no air on the Moon, and no air means mean no wind. How, then, does the flag stay up?

Before we get to the real answer, it's worth dispelling a common myth. If you ask why the flag stays up, a lot of people try to claim that "there's no gravity on the Moon." But it's pretty obvious that they're wrong. The fact that the astronauts are walking on the Moon, rather than floating away, demonstrates that there *is* gravity on the Moon. The only difference between gravity on Earth and gravity on the Moon is that the Moon's gravity is weaker.

So what's the real reason that the flag stays up? Simple — it had a stiff telescoping pole inserted into its top edge, which the astronauts extended as they unfurled the flag.

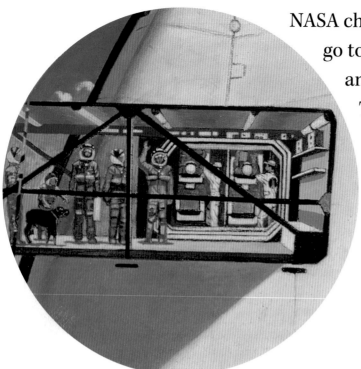

NASA chose six experienced astronauts to go to the Moon with Max. Since Max and Tori made such a good team, Tori got to go along too.

So the crew of seven humans and one dog blasted off into space.

Wings in Space?

Airplanes and rockets both fly, but in very different ways. Airplanes need wings to fly. Airplane wings have special shapes so that, when the airplane goes fast enough, air pushes up under the wings harder than it pushes down over them. The extra upward push creates what we call *lift*, allowing the airplane to fly. Pilots can adjust flaps on the wings to increase or decrease the lift, making the plane go up or down.

Wings are useless in space, because there is no air to provide lift. That is why space-ships need rocket engines. (The Space Shuttle used its wings only for landing on Earth.)

Within a few hours, they were docked at the Space Station, where their moonship was waiting. After lunch on the Space Station, the crew boarded the moonship.

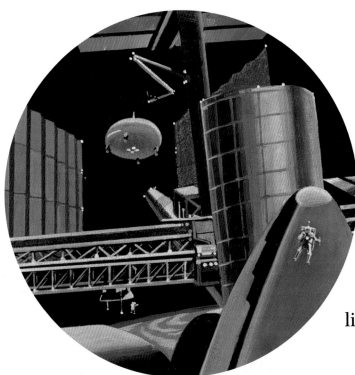

The crew fired the moonship's rocket engines to gain speed, leaving Earth orbit. Once on their way, they turned off the engines and coasted toward the Moon. The trip took a little more than two days.

Rockets

A rocket works by shooting a stream of hot gas out its back, which makes the rocket itself go forward. It's the same basic idea as when you inflate a balloon and let it go without tying the end: the balloon flies forward as air shoots out its end. Of course, the rocket engine offers much more power and much more control than the balloon.

Soon, the Moon loomed large in the window, with the Earth far behind. The crew turned the ship around, so firing the rocket engines slowed it down. As the moonship neared the surface, the blast from its engines kicked up a cloud of moon dust. Then it settled gently onto the Moon.

It may look like rockets "push off" the ground, but they don't; their power comes from shooting the hot gas out the back. In fact, the ground (and air in our atmosphere) gets in the way of the streaming gas, so rocket engines perform better in space than on Earth.

Amazingly, spaceships don't even need rocket engines, except to speed up, slow down, or turn. In space, where there's no air to create friction or drag, spaceships can coast forever without engine power. That's why the moonship can cut its engines once on its way to the Moon. It's also why spaceships and satellites don't need fuel to remain in orbit around the Earth, as long as their orbits are high enough to be fully above the Earth's atmosphere.

The same idea explains why the Moon needs no fuel to keep orbiting the Earth and why the Earth and other planets need no fuel to keep orbiting the Sun. With no air to slow them down, moons and planets can orbit forever.

Spacesuits

You probably know that spacesuits allow astronauts to carry air with them. But did you ever wonder why spacesuits are so thick?

One reason is to protect astronauts from temperature extremes. With no air to moderate temperatures in space, it gets very hot in sunlight and very cold in shadow — the difference from light to shadow on the Moon can be 400°F (220°C)! Spacesuits must have heating and cooling systems to keep temperatures steady for the astronauts inside.

A second reason is to protect astronauts from dangerous radiation from the Sun, such as ultraviolet and X rays. On Earth, our atmosphere protects us from this radiation. In space, astronauts outside their spaceships must rely on their spacesuits to block this radiation. Other reasons for spacesuit thickness include maintaining the air pressure inside them and protecting astronauts from high-speed particles in space.

Spacesuits also allow astronauts to communicate, because they contain built-in radios. Despite what you may have heard in science fiction movies, sound cannot travel through empty space. Space is always silent, and even explosions make no sound in space. When we hear astronauts talking in space, we are actually hearing voices transmitted by the radios in their spacesuits.

Max was so excited about reaching the Moon that the crew had a hard time getting his spacesuit on. It took three of them just to hold Max while the others pulled the spacesuit over his legs. Tori made sure that Max's tail went in the right place. Then they closed all the buckles and attached his helmet. Finally, they checked carefully to make sure that the spacesuit was airtight.

have seen the look on his face! He went much higher and farther than he had expected. It also took him much longer to come down than he was used to on Earth. Tori watched out the window and said,

"That's one giant leap for a dog!"

Weak Gravity

Have you ever wondered *why* objects fall to the ground? The answer is *gravity*, which pulls everything on Earth downward. If you jump up, gravity pulls you back down. It keeps pulling even when you are on the ground, which is what gives you weight.

On Earth, the strength of gravity is about the same everywhere. But gravity is different on other worlds. Gravity on the Moon is about six times weaker than on the Earth, so you would weigh only about one-sixth as much on the Moon as you do on Earth. Everything else weighs less on the Moon too, so you could lift big objects that would be too heavy to lift on Earth, and throw things much higher and farther.

The Moon's weaker gravity also means that everything falls back to the ground more slowly than it does on Earth. That, along with reduced weight, is why astronauts find it easier to bound than to walk on the Moon. It is also why Max got such a big surprise when he made his first Moon leap.

The Airless Moon

Max noticed a lot of strange things on the Moon, many of which occur because the Moon has no atmosphere. That's why astronauts (and astrodogs!) must bring their own air with them in their spaceships and spacesuits, and why their spacesuits must protect them from dangerous radiation. But the lack of air has other effects too.

On Earth, the atmosphere creates *pressure*, without which the oceans would boil even at low temperatures. The Moon's lack of atmosphere means no pressure and therefore no liquid water. With no air and no liquid water, there is no life on the Moon. That's why Max could not find any sticks.

On Earth, wind and rain cause *erosion* that usually erases footprints within a few days. There is no wind or rain on the Moon, which is why astronaut footprints — and Max's paw prints — can remain unchanged for centuries.

On Earth, air holds warmth and spreads sunlight into shadows. Because there is no air on the Moon, the shadows are extremely cold and dark. That's why Max couldn't see anything and his head got very cold when he looked into the shadow behind a rock.

On Earth, the atmosphere spreads the Sun's light all over the sky, making the day-time sky bright and blue and hiding the dim light of stars. On the Moon, the lack of air means the sky is blacker than the darkest night. If you look away from the Sun and the bright lunar surface, you can see stars even in the daytime on the Moon.

For posterity, the astronauts fenced off the spot where Max made his first paw prints on the Moon. There is no wind or rain on the Moon, so those paw prints are still there today, even though it has been many years since Max's first Moon trip.

Max thought it would be fun to play with a stick. He didn't see any, so he decided to look behind a big rock. But when he poked his head into the rock's shadow, he couldn't see a thing. It was darker than the darkest night, and cold, too.

Max leaped backward with a look of surprise and worry. Tori bounded over to calm him down.

"It's OK Max. You're a good dog. Just try to stay out of the shadows. Anyway, you won't find any sticks on the Moon. Nothing lives here, so there aren't any trees."

"Here, I brought a Frisbee to play with."

Moon Dust

Max and the astronauts leave footprints because most of the Moon's surface is covered by a thin layer of powdery "moon dust." Beneath this thin layer, the dust is so tightly packed that it feels solid, and below that is solid rock.

You might wonder why the Moon has a dusty surface. The answer goes back to its lack of air. The dust is basically crushed rock — rock that has been pulverized by impacts of sand-sized particles from space. On Earth, these types of particles burn up in our atmosphere as "shooting stars," or *meteors*. On the Moon, the lack of air means the particles crash to the ground at speeds many times faster than bullets, so that each impact creates a tiny bit of dust. Although these *micrometeorite* impacts are quite rare in any particular place, over billions of years there have been enough of them to give the Moon a dusty surface.

Moon dust may look like dark sand, but the grains are jagged-edged and sharp (because there's no erosion from wind or rain to smooth them out). They also carry static electricity that makes them stick to almost anything. In fact, moon dust created a lot of problems for the Apollo astronauts, because it got just about everywhere and could jam up equipment. One challenge of future Moon missions will be finding a way to deal with the problems of Moon dust.

Buzz Aldrin took this photo of a footprint during the Apollo 11 mission.

19

Tori got off a good throw, even though her big spacesuit glove made it a little hard to hold the Frisbee. Max bounded after it. But it didn't curve the way Max expected, and he missed it by a lot.

Tori quickly realized why Max was confused. He didn't know that objects move differently when there's no air. Tori picked up a rock and pulled a feather from her pack. "Look at this feather," she explained to Max. "On Earth, the air would make it float gently to the ground. But there's no air here on the Moon, so it falls just like the rock."

Falling Without Air

Tori's demonstration with the feather and rock reveals an important fact about gravity: without air to affect motion, all objects would fall to the ground at the same rate.

This fact surprises many people, because on Earth we are always surrounded by air. Indeed, this fact about gravity was discovered only about 400 years ago, by the famous Italian scientist named Galileo.

You can test this fact for yourself. If you drop a rock and a flat piece of paper, the rock falls rapidly while the paper wafts gently to the ground. But if you wad the paper into a tight ball, so that air cannot affect it so much, the rock and the ball of paper fall together.

By the way, Tori's demonstration with the rock and feather is based on a real demonstration conducted by Apollo 15 astronaut Dave Scott; the only difference is that astronaut Scott used a hammer he had brought with him instead of a rock. You can watch the video of Scott's demonstration at www.BigKidScience.com/max_moon.

Tori picked up the Frisbee and threw it again. This time Max knew what to do. She threw it very high, so Max had time to get under it. He stopped and turned around to see the Frisbee coming down. He was perfectly positioned for the catch.

There was only one problem...

Frisbees and Curve Balls on the Moon

The effects of air are even more dramatic for Frisbees and other flying toys. Their fancy curves and turns are possible only because of the way air pushes against them. Without air, a Frisbee's path through the sky would be as simple as the path of a thrown rock. That's why Max was surprised by Tori's first throw; he expected it to curve like it would have on Earth.

Air swirling around a fast-moving baseball is also what makes curve balls possible. Outside on the Moon, even the best major league pitcher would have no curve ball.

Of course, if you played inside an air-filled Moon colony, Frisbees and baseballs would behave as they do on Earth — except that because of the weaker gravity, they could be thrown higher and farther and would remain airborne longer.

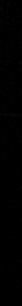

Rock Science

Have you ever wondered why scientists are so interested in rocks? The answer is that we can learn a lot from rocks, because all rocks have a history.

Like everything else that we can touch and feel, rocks are made from microscopic *atoms* and *molecules*. These atoms and molecules can move all around in a gas like air or a liquid like water or molten lava, but they are locked into place in solids like ice and rock. As a result, careful study of rocks can tell us about how and where they formed.

Amazingly, we can even learn exactly *when* a rock solidified. Many rocks contain atoms that are *radioactive*, which means they tend to change into other types of atoms over time. For example, atoms of uranium eventually transform into atoms of lead. Scientists can measure the rate at which these transformations occur, and then use their understanding of these rates to determine the age of a rock.

These kinds of studies have taught us that the Sun, Earth, and planets were all born about 4½ billion years ago in a huge, swirling cloud of gas. Moreover, careful comparison of Earth rocks and Moon rocks has led to our best guess about how the Moon formed: Scientists suspect that the Moon was born shortly after Earth formed, when a gigantic asteroid slammed into the young Earth, blasting its outer layers into space. Gravity then pulled some of this material together to make the Moon. By collecting and studying more Moon rocks, we may someday learn whether this idea is really correct.

next few days. They collected moon rocks for science, and they set up telescopes to study distant planets and stars. But most of all, they loved gazing upward at the Earth, which seemed to hang in one place in the sky.

Soon, the longer shadows told Max and the crew that darkness was coming. It was time to leave.

Once everyone was aboard the moonship, Max and Tori waved goodbye to the Moon, and the crew closed the door. They fired the rocket engines and blasted off the Moon.

Just twelve days after leaving the Earth, Max, Tori, and the rest of the astronauts were back on the Space Station. Then a space shuttle took them home.

Day and Night on the Moon

We have day and night because the Earth spins, or *rotates*, once each day.

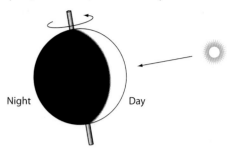

The Moon rotates too, but more slowly: the Moon's "day" lasts about a month instead of 24 hours. On the Moon, you'd have about two weeks from sunrise to sunset, followed by two weeks of night.

The Moon's rotation is special in another way: it is just the right speed so that the Moon always keeps the same face toward Earth. This special rotation is not a coincidence; it is a natural consequence of the way gravity affects the Earth and Moon. Looking from the Moon's surface, the Earth would seem to hang in your sky, always in about the same place and neither rising nor setting. But as it hangs in the sky, you'd see the Earth go through a monthly cycle of phases, from new to full and back again, just as we see phases of the Moon from Earth; we see a crescent Earth on page 22. You'd also see the Earth slowly rotating, completing a full turn once every 24 hours.

By the way, some people wonder how Max and Tori and the crew took a space shuttle home when NASA's Space Shuttles have been retired. The answer is that a "shuttle" can be any vehicle that travels between two places, such as Earth and a space station.

23

Why Build a Moon Colony?

A Moon colony would be a great place to visit, with beautiful views and the fun of playing in weak gravity. But a Moon colony could also offer important benefits.

Moon rocks contain many valuable metals. Some people imagine mining the Moon to send these metals back to Earth, and we could certainly use them to build our Moon colony, as well as to build spaceships for exploring the rest of the solar system. The Moon's soil also contains a trapped gas, called helium-3, which is very rare on Earth. Some scientists believe this gas could be used as fuel for *fusion* power plants that would generate abundant, safe, and clean energy.

The Moon is also valuable scientifically. Moon rocks can teach us about the history of our solar system, and learning about the Moon's geology may help us better understand volcanoes and earthquakes on Earth. Astronomy from the Moon might provide even greater scientific benefit. The lack of air means that telescopes on the Moon have a clearer view of the universe than telescopes on Earth. And while the same clear view can be obtained with telescopes in space (such as the Hubble Space Telescope), it would be much easier for astronauts to build and operate large telescopes on the Moon's solid surface.

Of course, the greatest value of a Moon colony may come from the way it could inspire children to work hard and fulfill their dreams. As the dedication page states, dreams and effort may someday help us live in a world as wonderful as the one we imagine in this book.

Back on Earth, billions of people watched Max's trip on the news. Everyone talked about it. Some grownups said the trip wasn't worth the money it cost.

But children understood the excitement of it all. They asked their parents to help send Max to the Moon again — but this time to build a big colony where many children could go visit him and learn about the universe.

Atmospheres and Telescopes

We depend on Earth's atmosphere for survival, but the atmosphere creates two major problems for telescopes.

First, do you remember the song *Twinkle, Twinkle, Little Star*? Twinkling may be beautiful, but it blurs pictures taken with telescopes on Earth. To understand why, drop a coin to the bottom of a glass of water. Stir the water gently and the coin will look like it is moving even while it is actually still, because you are looking at it through moving water. In much the same way, we see stars twinkle only because we view them through the moving air in the Earth's atmosphere. Viewed from space, starlight is steady as can be.

To understand the second problem, think about a dog whistle. Dogs can hear it, but people can't. Just as there are sounds we cannot hear, there are some kinds of light we cannot see. However, we can still make pictures from this light by using special telescopes and cameras. The pictures show us what things would look like *if* our eyes could see this light. These special pictures can reveal details about the universe that would otherwise remain invisible. Earth's atmosphere blocks most of the invisible light, so we can study it only with telescopes in space or on the Moon.

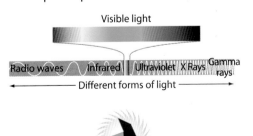

Visible light

| Radio waves | Infrared | Ultraviolet | X Rays | Gamma rays |

Different forms of light

25

The University of the Moon

Would *you* like to go to college on the Moon? This painting shows one vision of what a colony that houses a University of the Moon might look like.

As the story says, the colony would be filled with air, and in principle we could make it feel very Earth-like inside, with plants and ponds and other things to make it feel like home. Of course, you'd still be living in the Moon's weak gravity, so at the basketball court you'd see students jumping completely over the hoops!

You might wonder how we'd get all that stuff there. We'd need to bring plants and organic soil from Earth, but structures could be built with materials mined from the Moon itself, and scientists have found ways in which we could extract oxygen from Moon rocks to make air. The biggest challenge would probably be water, but we might even be able to get that from the Moon. There are tiny amounts of water locked up in Moon rocks, and scientists recently discovered larger amounts frozen as ice in craters near the Moon's north and south poles.

All in all, if we really made the effort, we could probably build a Moon colony in a decade or two. In that case, some of today's children might really be able to go to college on the Moon, and their parents could come visit at spring break!

The children were so convincing that all the nations of the world decided to work together to build a big, domed colony on the Moon.

The domes covered homes, offices, and, of course, the University of the Moon. They were filled with air so that no one needed a spacesuit inside. Food grew in greenhouses and water was carefully recycled.

Outside the domes, astronauts built great telescopes to observe the universe. Students and scientists made important new discoveries almost every day.

The building of the Moon Colony also changed a lot of things back on Earth.

Children tried to learn more in school, in hopes that they might get to attend the University of the Moon. Grownups saved their money for tourist trips to the Moon.

Most importantly, the beautiful views of Earth from the Moon made everyone realize that we all share a small and precious planet.

27

Of course, none of it would have happened without Max.

Max was glad that he had been so helpful. But he was not the type of dog to stop at that.

28

It's a big universe out there. Where would he go next?

Understanding the Phases of the Moon

Do you want to know *why* the Moon goes through phases? It's easy to understand with a simple demonstration.

Take a ball outside on a sunny day. Pretend the ball is the Moon and your head is the Earth. Hold the ball at arm's length and spin slowly around (always turning to your left), so that the ball goes around you like the Moon orbits around Earth. The half of the ball facing the Sun is always sunlit and the other half is always dark, but the face of the ball that *you* see will go through phases as you turn.

Start by holding the ball toward the Sun. You'll see only the dark half of the ball, so this represents "new ball." As you begin to turn, you'll see the ball go through waxing phases. First, you'll see a sunlit crescent. After you've made a quarter turn, you'll see a face of the ball that is half sunlit and half dark — "first quarter ball." Next, you'll see a "gibbous ball" that is more than half full, and when you are facing opposite the Sun you'll see "full ball." You'll then see the waning phases as you continue around.

We see Moon phases for the same reason. The Moon always has a daylight half and a dark half, but the phase we see depends on where it is located in its orbit around Earth. The diagram with Tori and Max shows the point in the Moon's orbit where we see each phase, and the photos show what the phases look like.

Challenge: When we see a new moon, what phase of Earth would be seen by people on the Moon? (For the answer, visit www.BigKidScience.com/max_moon.)

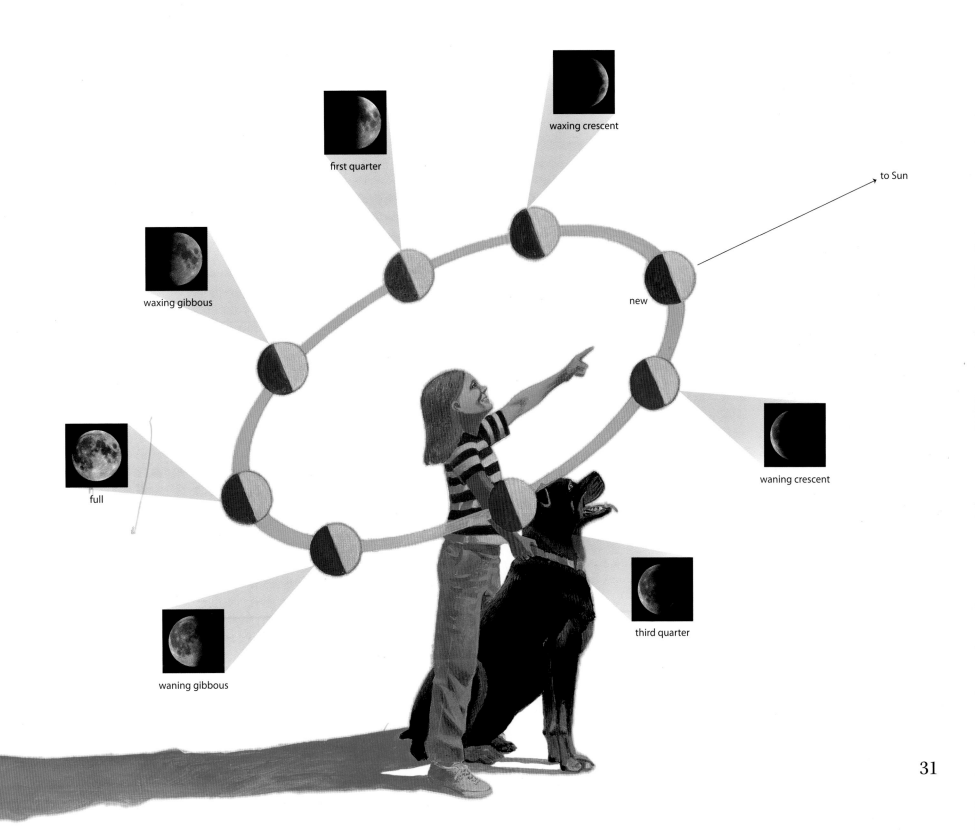

first quarter

waxing crescent

to Sun

waxing gibbous

new

full

waning crescent

waning gibbous

third quarter

About Max

The real Max was a 120-pound (55-kilogram) Rottweiler who lived with the author and his family. Max was friendly as could be, and his playful antics provided the inspiration for this book. He was best-known for his merry-go-round trick, in which he made a playground merry-go-round spin by running around it while pushing on it with his paws. Once it was spinning fast, he'd jump on and off — always being careful not to bang into any children riding with him. (See the video at www.BigKidScience.com/maxvideo/.) He's also the only dog we've ever met who wouldn't eat a steak unless you first cut it into small pieces for him.

Max in Space

Max was made an honorary crew member on the final flight of the Space Shuttle Discovery, during which astronaut Alvin Drew read *Max Goes to the Moon* aloud from orbit. Learn more and watch the video at www.BigKidScience.com/max_in_space.

The *Max Goes to the Moon* Planetarium Show

Don't miss the *Max Goes to the Moon* planetarium show, now showing at planetariums around the world. This critically acclaimed show was produced at the Fiske Planetarium in Boulder, Colorado, with support from NASA's Lunar Science Institute. For more information and to learn how you can stream a flat screen version of the show, please visit www.BigKidScience.com/planetariumshow.